Possum Come a-Knockin'

by NANCY VAN LAAN

Illustrated by GEORGE BOOTH

E.G. Sherburne S

DRAGONFLY BOOKS™

Alfred A. Knopf • New York

For John, Celia, Rachel, Jessica, and
all my kinfolk way down South   —N. V. L.

To Grover Babcock, my brother-in-law,
who loves critters   —G. B.

DRAGONFLY BOOKS™ PUBLISHED BY ALFRED A. KNOPF, INC.

Text copyright © 1990 by Nancy Van Laan
Illustrations copyright © 1990 by George Booth

http://www.randomhouse.com/

Library of Congress Catalog Card Number: 88-12751
ISBN: 0-679-83468-0
First Dragonfly Books™ edition: September 1992

Printed in Singapore 15 14 13 12 11 10 9 8

Possum come a-knockin'
at the door, at the door.
Possum come a-knockin'
at the door.

Granny was a-sittin'
and a-rockin' and a-knittin'
when a possum come a-knockin'
at the door.

Ma was busy cookin'
in the kitchen makin' taters
when a possum come a-knockin'
at the door.

Pa was busy fixin'
and a-bangin' and a-poundin'
when a possum come a-knockin'
at the door.

Pappy was a-whittlin',
makin' play toys for the baby,
when a possum come a-knockin'
at the door.

Sis was tossin' Baby
while Pappy was a-whittlin'
when a possum come a-knockin'
at the door.

Brother was untanglin'
all the twiny line for fishin'
while Sis was tossin' Baby
and Pappy was a-whittlin'

and Pa was busy fixin'
and Ma was busy cookin'
and Granny was a-knittin'
when a possum come a-knockin'
at the door.

Coon-dawg was a-twitchin'
and a-scratchin' in the corner
when a possum come a-knockin'
at the door.

Tom-cat started sniffin'
and a-spittin' and a-hissin'
when a possum come a-knockin'
at the door.

"What's that?" Sis said.
"Don't know," Brother said.
"What's that?" Pa said.
"Don't know," Granny said.
"But that cat!" she said.
"That cat oughter go!"

Then dawg started sniffin'
and a-pawin' and a-growlin'
while the cat, tail a-twitchin',
was a-hissin' and a-howlin',

makin' Granny stop a-knittin'
and Pappy stop a-whittlin'
and Baby start a-fussin',
Sis and Brother start a-cussin',
'cause a li'l ol' possum
was a-knockin'
at the door.

"What's that?" Granny said.
"Don't know," Pappy said.
"What's that?" Ma said.
"Don't know," Pa said.
   Then I creepy-crossed the floor
   and peeked under the door.

"It's a possum come a-knockin'
     on the door!" I said.
"It's a possum come a-knockin'
     on the door!"

Then Brother came a-leapin'
and Sis came a-runnin'
and Baby came a-crawlin'
and dawg started howlin'
and Pappy was a-chucklin'
and Granny's eyes was twinklin'
as Ma followed Pa to the door.

"Now, hush!" Pa said.
"Now, hush!" Ma said.
And slowly Pa opened
up the door.
"Now, y'all stop your hollerin',
your fussin', and your cussin',
'cause there's nothin'
that's a-knockin' at the door."

"No possum?" Pappy said.
"No possum," Pa said.
"No possum?" Granny said.
"No possum," Ma said.
  Then we all started doin'
  like before.

Granny was a-sittin'
while Pappy was a-whittlin'.
Ma was a-cookin'
while Pa was a-fixin'.

Brother was untanglin'
while Sis was tossin' Baby.
Coon-dawg was a-scratchin'
while Tom-cat was a-lickin'.

And I was just a-sittin'
and a-lookin' out the winder
when I saw what I saw
scoot up the old oak tree.

A possum was a-scootin'
and a-scramblin' and a-danglin'.
That possum that was knockin'
made a fool out of me!

ALLOSAURUS

INTRODUCING DINOSAURS

BY SUSAN H. GRAY · ILLUSTRATED BY ROBERT SQUIER

South Huntington Pub. Lib.
145 Pidgeon Hill Rd.
Huntington Sta., N.Y. 11746

The Child's World®

Published by The Child's World®
1980 Lookout Drive • Mankato, MN 56003-1705
800-599-READ • www.childsworld.com

ACKNOWLEDGMENTS

The Child's World®: Mary Berendes, Publishing Director
The Design Lab: Kathleen Petelinsek, Art Direction and Design;
Victoria Stanley and Anna Petelinsek, Page Production
Editorial Directions: E. Russell Primm, Editor; Lucia Raatma, Copy Editor;
Dina Rubin, Proofreader; Tim Griffin, Indexer

PHOTO CREDITS

©Juliengrondon/Dreamstime.com: cover and 2–3; ©Kevin Ebi/Alamy: 8
© Martin Shields/Alamy: 10–11; ©Michael S. Yamashita/Corbis: 11 (right);
© Sinclair Stammers/Photo Researchers, Inc.: 12; © Getty Images/Hulton
Archive: 16 (top); ©American Museum of Natural History; © Paul Carter/
Alamy: 18–19; © Albert Copley/Visuals Unlimited: 19 (right)

LIBRARY OF CONGRESS CATALOGING-IN-PUBLICATION DATA

Gray, Susan Heinrichs.
  Allosaurus / by Susan H. Gray; illustrated by Robert Squier.
      p. cm. —(Introducing dinosaurs) (What was Allosaurus?—What did
Allosaurus look like?—Who was big Al?—What did Allosaurus do all day?
—How do we know about Allosaurus?)
  Includes bibliographical references and index.
  ISBN 978-1-60253-234-2 (lib. bound: alk. paper)
  1. Allosaurus—Juvenile literature. I. Squier, Robert, ill. II. Title.
  QE862.S3G6912 2009
  567.912—dc22   2009001620

Printed in the United States of America
Mankato, Minnesota
July, 2010
PA02066

TABLE OF CONTENTS

WHAT WAS ALLOSAURUS?

Allosaurus (al-luh-SAWR-uss) was a big, meat-eating dinosaur. It lived 150 million years ago. It was one of the largest predators that ever lived.

Allosaurus was longer than a school bus. It weighed as much as a hundred first-graders!

Allosaurus was gigantic! It had no trouble fighting other dinosaurs.

4

WHAT DID ALLOSAURUS LOOK LIKE?

Allosaurus had a huge head. It had bumps and knobs on its face. It had a bony shelf above each eye. Its mouth was loaded with sharp, curved teeth. They were good for tearing up meat.

We know that Allosaurus was a meat eater. Meat-eating dinosaurs had pointed teeth for tearing meat.

Allosaurus had little arms. It used them to hold its food. This dinosaur walked around on two mighty legs. Its fingers and toes had sharp claws.

Allosaurus had a long tail. It also had very heavy bones. They held up an enormous dinosaur!

A person's hand (above) seems tiny inside an Allosaurus dinosaur track near Potash, Utah. Allosaurus (right) walked on two legs. This kept its hands free for attacking enemies.

6

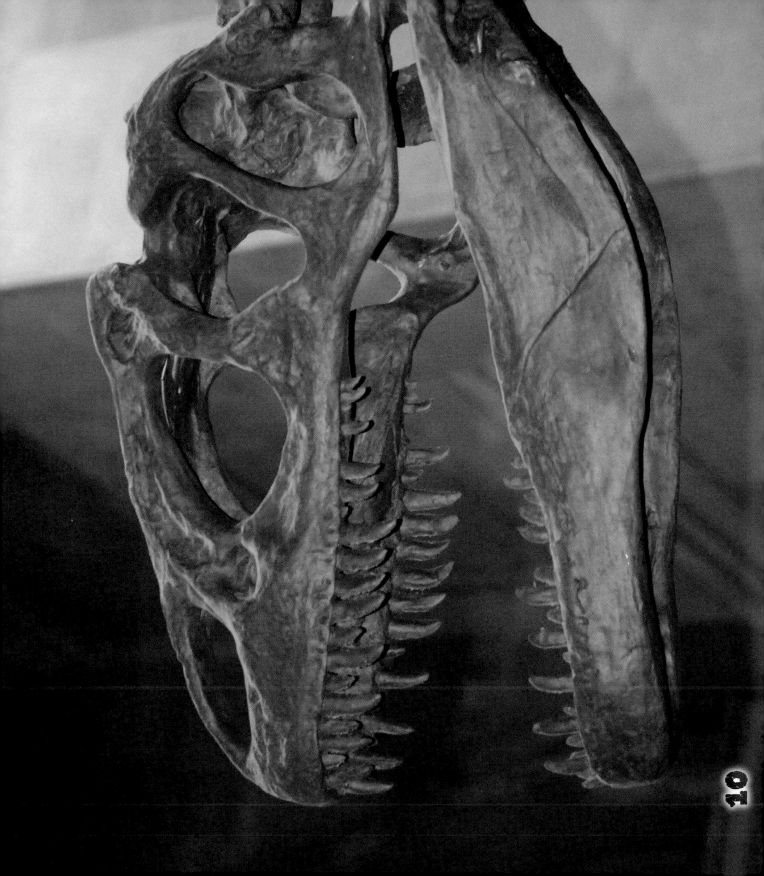

WHO WAS BIG AL?

Scientists have discovered many Allosaurus fossils. They have found bones, teeth, and claws. About 20 years ago, they found a terrific skeleton. It was from a young Allosaurus.

The fossilized bones and claws of Allosaurus have helped scientists learn a great deal about the dinosaur.

Scientists took a long look at the skeleton. They said the young dinosaur had a very tough life. It had broken its ribs and tailbones. Its fingers and toes had infections. Its shoulder and hips had been damaged. It probably limped around. The scientists named this dinosaur Big Al.

Fossils (above) are the main way scientists study the lives of dinosaurs. Smaller dinosaurs such as this Compsognathus (komp-sug-NATH-uss) were no match for the mighty Allosaurus (right).

14

WHAT DID ALLOSAURUS DO ALL DAY?

Allosaurus usually just hunted, ate, and slept. Scientists think it was not a very speedy runner. It probably did not race after its food. Instead, it went after big, slow dinosaurs. Perhaps Allosaurus followed **herds**. Maybe it ate dinosaurs that became sick or died.

Allosaurus did not fear many other dinosaurs. It would attack whole groups of slow-moving dinosaurs, such as these Braciosaurus (brake-ee-ah-SAWR-uss).

HOW DO WE KNOW ABOUT *ALLOSAURUS*?

Years ago, someone discovered the first Allosaurus fossil. Everyone thought it was a horse's hoof!

Finally, somebody realized the fossil was from a dinosaur.

This Allosaurus fossilized leg bone (above), found in the 1860s, is taller than an adult man. Over the years, scientists have even discovered whole Allosaurus skeletons (right).

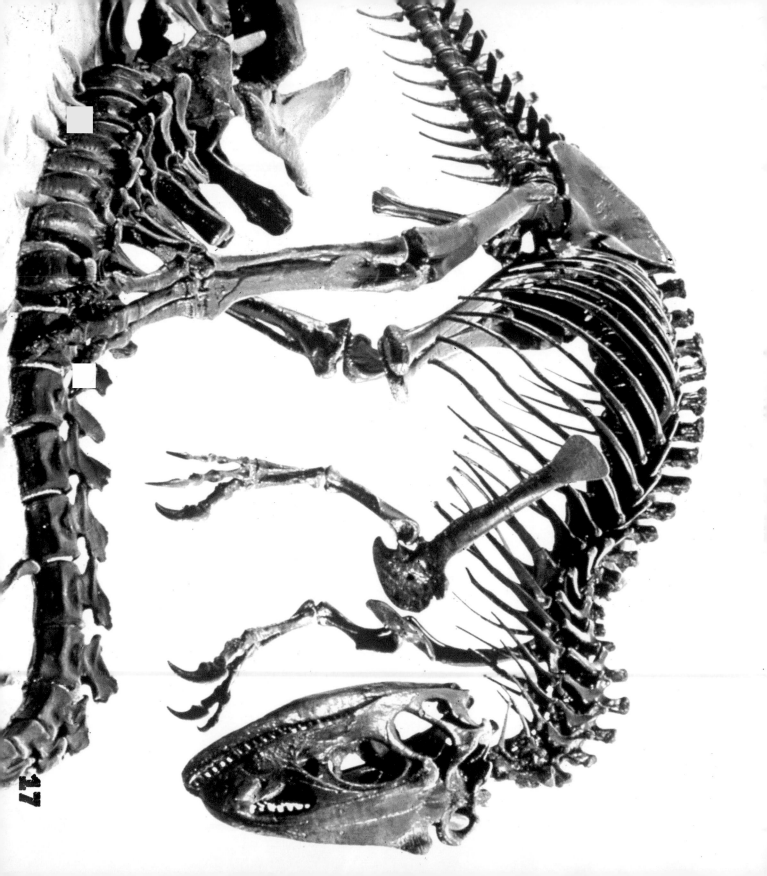

Since then, scientists have found hundreds of Allosaurus fossils. They have found its tooth marks on other dinosaurs' bones. They have studied Big Al's injuries. Now we know plenty about Allosaurus!

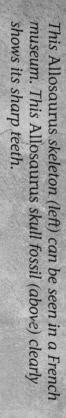

This Allosaurus skeleton (left) can be seen in a French museum. This Allosaurus skull fossil (above) clearly shows its sharp teeth.

WHERE HAVE ALLOSAURUS BONES BEEN FOUND?

ASIA

EUROPE

AFRICA

AUSTRALIA

Australia

Tanzania

Indian Ocean

Southern Ocean

Portugal

Colorado

Wyoming

South Dakota

Oklahoma

Montana

NORTH AMERICA

Utah

New Mexico

SOUTH AMERICA

Atlantic Ocean

Pacific Ocean

Map Key

Where *Allosaurus* bones have been found

Where possible *Allosaurus* fossils have been found

20

WHO FINDS THE BONES?

Fossil hunters find dinosaur bones. Some fossil hunters are scientists. Others are people who hunt fossils for fun. They go to areas where dinosaurs once lived. They find bones in rocky places, in mountainsides, and in deserts.

When fossil hunters discover dinosaur bones, they get busy. They use picks to chip rocks away from the fossils.

They use small brushes to sweep off any dirt. They take pictures of the fossils. They also write notes about where the fossils were found. They want to remember everything!

Fossil hunters use many tools to dig up fossils. It is very important to use the right tools so the fossils do not get damaged.

GLOSSARY

Allosaurus (*al-luh-SAWR-uss*) Allosaurus was a big, meat-eating dinosaur.

fossils (*FOSS-ullz*) Fossils are preserved parts of plants and animals that died long ago.

herds (*HURDZ*) Herds are groups of animals that travel together.

infections (*in-FEK-shunz*) Infections are places on the body that are sore and full of germs.

predators (*PRED-ah-turz*) Predators are animals that hunt and eat other animals.

scientists (*SY-un-tists*) Scientists are people who study how things work through observations and experiments.

skeleton (*SKEL-uh-tun*) The skeleton is the set of bones in a person or animal's body.

BOOKS

Birch, Robin. *Meat-eating Dinosaurs.*
New York: Chelsea House Publishers, 2008.

Cole, Stephen. *Allosaurus: The Life and Death of Big Al.*
New York: Dutton Juvenile, 2001.

My Terrific Dinosaur Book.
New York: DK Publishing, 2008.

Stille, Darlene R. *Allosaurus.*
Vero Beach, FL: Rourke Publishing, 2007.

WEB SITES

Visit our Web site for lots of links about Allosaurus:

CHILDSWORLD.COM/LINKS

Note to Parents, Teachers, and Librarians: We routinely verify our Web links to make sure they are safe, active sites—so encourage your readers to check them out!

ABOUT THE AUTHOR

Susan Gray has written more than ninety books for children. She especially likes to write about animals. Susan lives in Cabot, Arkansas, with her husband, Michael, and many pets.

ABOUT THE ILLUSTRATOR

Robert Squier has been drawing dinosaurs ever since he could hold a crayon. Today, instead of using crayons, he uses pencils, paint, and the computer. Robert lives in New Hampshire with his wife, Jessica, and a house full of dinosaur toys. *Stegosaurus* is his favorite dinosaur.

INDEX